DROHOBYCZ, DROHOBYCZ

AND OTHER STORIES

True Tales from the Holocaust and Life After

HENRYK GRYNBERG

<small>Translated from the Polish by Alicia Nitecki
Edited by Theodosia Robertson</small>

PENGUIN BOOKS

PENGUIN BOOKS

Published by the Penguin Group

Penguin Putnam Inc., 375 Hudson Street, New York, New York 10014, U.S.A.

Penguin Books Ltd, 80 Strand, London WC2R 0RL, England

Penguin Books Australia Ltd, 250 Camberwell Road, Camberwell, Victoria 3124, Australia

Penguin Books Canada Ltd, 10 Alcorn Avenue, Toronto, Ontario, Canada M4V 3B2

Penguin Books India (P) Ltd, 11 Community Centre,

Panchsheel Park, New Delhi – 110 017, India

Penguin Books (N.Z.) Ltd, Cnr Rosedale and Airborne Roads,

Albany, Auckland, New Zealand

Penguin Books (South Africa) (Pty) Ltd, 24 Sturdee Avenue,

Rosebank, Johannesburg 2196, South Africa

Penguin Books Ltd, Registered Offices: Harmondsworth, Middlesex, England

First published in Penguin Books 2002

10 9 8 7 6 5 4 3 2 1

Translation copyright © Henryk Grynberg, 2002
All rights reserved

Drohobycz, Drohobycz originally published in Polish by Wydawnictwo W.A.B., Warsaw
Copyright © Henryk Grynberg, 1997

The following selections, translated by Alicia Nitecki, were previously published: "Brother in Volhynia" in *Chicago Review;* "Drohobycz, Drohobycz" in *The Massachusetts Review;* and "Escape from Boryslaw" in *Midstream.*

PUBLISHER'S NOTE
In this collection of stories Henryk Grynberg uses the art of fiction to cast new light on the horrifying facts of Holocaust.

LIBRARY OF CONGRESS CATALOGING-IN-PUBLICATION DATA
Grynberg, Henryk.
    [Short stories. English. Selections]
    Drohobycz, Drohobycz and other stories : true tales from the Holocaust and life after /
Henryk Grynberg ; translated from the Polish by Alicia Nitecki ; edited by Theodosia
Robertson.
        p. cm.
    ISBN 0-14-200165-1
    1. Grynberg, Henryk—Translations into English. 2. Holocaust, Jewish
(1939–1945)—Fiction. I. Nitecki, Alicia, 1942– II. Robertson, Theodosia S.
III. Title.
PG7166.R86 A26 2002
891.8'537—dc21   2002028995

Printed in the United States of America
Set in Adobe Garamond / Designed by M. Paul

CONTENTS